THE WORLD IS YOURS

MICROFICTIONS

RAN WALKER

ISBN: 9781020001192 (Paperback)
ISBN: 9781020001185 (Ebook)

First Edition

10 9 8 7 6 5 4 3 2

www.45alternate.com
45 Alternate Press, LLC

CONTENTS

For Elle,
who continues to be
my number one cheerleader

PREFACE

I didn't plan to write this book. In fact, as of March 2020, I could not focus my mind enough to write anything. My wife kept telling me to find my way back to writing as a way of coping with everything going on in the world, but it was a struggle. Then one day I had a breakthrough. Over the next couple of weeks I wrote *Bees + Things + Flowers*. But when I finished that book, it felt like the water was flowing too strongly to turn off the faucet, so I immediately began to write this book.

While listening to Nas's *Illmatic* album (from which the title of this collection is taken), I started to get more ideas, so I kept writing. What you are holding in your hands right now is a part of the same flow of water that produced *Bees + Things + Flowers*. With this book, however, I wanted not only to continue playing with my form and content, but with how I told the stories, as well.

Cue: *Dope Third Person Omniscient.*

What is *dope third person omniscient*? This is my personal take on how the vernacular and linguistical nuances of the author-as-omniscient-narrator operate on the telling of a story. This is similar to what Fitzgerald did with *The Great Gatsby* and what Junot Díaz did with *The Brief Wondrous Life of Oscar Wao*, but it's different in that this is not a "first person-mimicking-third person omniscient" type of thing. With dope third person, I have granted the voice of the omniscient narrator with a voice not unlike my own.

I got this idea back when I was in college and was at a party where a friend of mine did the grace before our meal. She conversed with God like they were longtime friends. There was a clear colloquialism that contrasted with all of the formalized praying I had heard growing up. Years later when I read Díaz's book, I felt a strong sense of the third person omniscient dopeness sliding through, before I discovered it was a first person book.

After that, I couldn't stop thinking about what it would look like for a work to commit to that laid-back style for an omniscient voice. So as I started drilling further into my microfiction, I decided that I wouldn't fight my impulses to write in a language that reflected my community a bit more. It actually took me 18 books to give myself permission to mess with third person omniscient and to stop feeling like, as a Black writer, that I had to prove I have an excellent command of the Queen's English. I no longer feel like I have to prove anything in that regard, so I plan to experiment more. Dope third person omniscient is one way of my doing that. I don't use it in all of my work, but it is definitely present in several of the stories included here.

So as you pour over these stories, I hope that you enjoy their content, as well as how I have chosen to tell them.

Ran Walker

THE WORLD IS YOURS

I know the dark delight of being strange, the penalty of difference in the crowd, the loneliness of wisdom among fools...

— CLAUDE MCKAY

1

THE COLLECTION

"You're trying to do too much with this collection," a friend told him. "I can't tell if you're writing jokes or poems or stories. This book is all over the place!"

He nodded. Maybe it was. But then there are so many different aspects to a person's personality, he figured. Maybe an eclectic collection of stories wasn't such a bad thing after all.

At least he hoped so.

CYPHER

BACK IN THE DAY "CYPHER" meant to spit mathematics, not even Supreme.

Others think it's all about secret codes. And maybe it is.

But when the emcees on the third floor of DuBois Hall form a midnight cypher and drop that Dilla instrumental, they're not spitting to impress each other. They're spitting to bring balance to the universe.

RADIO RAHEEM

WHEN SHAWN MET JADE, he thought she could be the Michelle to his Barrack. He even rented *Do the Right Thing* so they could watch it on their first date, too.

Things didn't go as he had planned, though. When the movie was over, they didn't make out. Instead, they drove around downtown imagining which business windows they would have thrown garbage cans through.

UNTRANSLATED

IAN HAD TAKEN Spanish in both high school and college, yet he could hardly understand it. But then one day, by chance, he came across a book by a brilliant Argentine writer and made the decision to read everything she'd ever written.

After devouring the handful of books translated into English, he learned that much of her canon remained untranslated.

So he returned to studying Spanish, and with each new lesson learned, he could feel a brick in the wall that stood between him and the writer fall permanently to the ground.

5

———

RE(TRO)SPECT

YEARS after he first crushed on her, he reached out to her over Facebook to reconnect. He was now an award-winning filmmaker, and she was a registered nurse. Both single and eager to see what was up.

After embracing, they sat down to dinner.

"You were pretty strange when we were growing up," she started by way of breaking the ice.

He nodded, immediately understanding why some crushes were best left in the past.

6

———

BUCKROE

TERRY CONTINUED to unwind his kite as it sailed higher and higher against the burnt orange of the sunset. Coltrane, his Lab, had given up chasing after it, choosing instead to trot along the coastline, its paws tracking the sand like musical notes.

That evening Terry would get his weekly phone call from his mother and how she worried about him being single at his age. But she couldn't see the sunset, the kite drifting toward the violet of dusk, or Coltrane nestling against his calves as he stood there with the sand between his toes.

He was just fine.

SCARLET

SHE LIVED her life in a state of constant improvisation. The music, jazz. The artwork, abstract. Her clothing, a freestyle of whatever was in her closet.

When he came into her life, he tried to put her in a box. What he failed to understand, though, was that her fluidity would eventually push her well beyond him—and everyone else who'd attempt to draw a line around her world and tell her to color within the lines.

SECOND CHANCES

IN THE WEEKS leading up to the class reunion, Wendell and Aisha had been talking feverishly on the phone. Facebook had turned into Face-Time, and now they would finally be in their hometown, exploring the "what if" that never came to pass while they were students.

Their memories rested gently on top of their present, almost seamless, as they listened to Dru Hill's "Beauty," remembering their adolescent yearning for each other.

Neither knew what would happen when they returned to their respective cities, but they were now reluctant to wait another ten years to tend to a flame that was clearly unextinguishable.

GRANT'S PROCRUSTES

(AFTER CHARLES CHESNUTT)

GRANT CONTINUED to talk about his mythological novel years after the only ten pages he'd written were ripped up by an angry girlfriend in an argument about him being *trifling*.

Three editors had asked to see it.

He'd taught several workshops based on the reputation it earned him.

He had no reason to ever finish the book.

Those who'd listened to him talk about it had already finished it for him.

THAT JURASSIC JOINT

THE MIXTAPE WAS a tree sap capturing our memories like insects, the songs becoming amber stones for our trunk jewelry. We were shielded against the heartbreakers—our bodies wrapped in teflon—but if you looked carefully at the amber, with our vulnerabilities perfectly captured, we were really only awaiting the right DJ to drill in, extract the DNA, and make a brand new joint.

RAE DAWN

AFTER THE RELATIONSHIP HAD ENDED, Gabe's boys asked him why he'd stayed in a relationship with a woman who clearly cared more about his money than him.

"I guess it's because she reminded me of that woman from *Commando*," he said.

Not understanding the reference, they decided to watch the movie. When they saw the woman playing opposite Schwarzenegger, Joe spoke for them all when he said, "Yep. I could see that."

QUARANTINE, DAY 12

HALFWAY THROUGH MASTURBATING with his girlfriend over FaceTime, Mark lost his connection.

No signal. At all.

He debated whether to finish or not, so he did.

When the connection returned moments later, his girlfriend asked if he was ready to resume.

"I've already finished," he said, resignedly.

"Wow," she responded, shaking her head. "Some things never change."

13

HAM

MY GIRLFRIEND THOUGHT she'd be slick and avoid the hog maws Big Mama was serving for lunch by simply lying and saying she didn't eat pork. That was a bad move.

All the meat in the house was pork Uncle Junior had brought home from his job at the slaughterhouse. Even if she didn't like the idea of hog maws or chitterlings, my girlfriend had ruled out the ham Big Mama planned to glaze and serve for dinner.

I told my girl she might want to walk back her statement—just a little. But she was terrified of all the country-ness enveloping her and refused, so I took her home.

When I made it back to Big Mama's, I listened to her tell me about Beulah Mae (who was still single) from the church—all while we ate that glorious ham.

THE BUSINESS OF HAPPINESS

By the time she reached the third book in the trilogy, she was questioning what had led her to write the series in the first place. She'd grown to hate the characters, was bored by the universe, and had even begun to think of the whole thing as a poor retelling of Homer's *Iliad*.

Writing used to be fun. Now she worried about book sales and advances. She often wished she could go back to those autumn days when she'd sit in a cafe and type on her MacBook.

Maybe she'd select a pseudonym and start over. That was a thing, right? No agents. No huge advances. Maybe a small press or something.

She was determined to make her sixteen-year-old self proud.

PROLIFIC

THE WILD-HAIRED GUY who introduced Cindy at the conference referred to her as "prolific," although she had only written one book.

Maybe he'd meant to say "profound" or "proficient"—or maybe "prodigious." She didn't think that either of those words truly fit, though. She wanted to ask him to explain it to her, but he was now sitting down so she could speak.

Taking the microphone, she nodded to him and said, "Thank you for that introduction. I only hope that one day I can live up to it."

CELEBRITY CRUSH

EVERY DECADE WAYMON fell in love with Janet Jackson all over again. He kept this to himself, though, fearing that one day his wife of twenty-five years would kick him out of their bed—or worse, admit she'd only married him because Denzel was unavailable.

AWKWARD

Neither of them knew how to kiss, their teeth clicking and clacking against the others, all a prelude to grinding their swollen parts together.

Looking back years later, one would call it a first love, the other a hot mess.

I WISH I WAS A LITTLE BIT TALLER

(AFTER SKEE-LO)

When Josh was in the eighth grade, he dropped a letter into Regina's backpack.

"Do you wanna be my girlfriend? Check Yes/No/Maybe So."

She never responded to the letter, but later that week, he heard from a friend that she let a basketball player from the 9th grade feel on her booty after the pep rally.

DEEP

"ELECTRIC RELAXATION."

"Let's Go Crazy."

"Buy U a Drank."

"The theme song from *Good Times*."

Lacy and Dillard went back and forth, passing the joint between themselves.

"Why do you think folks always fuck up those lyrics?"

"Maybe they're just riding the beat and they hear what they want to hear."

Satisfied with this bit of conversation, they stared out into the night sky, in search of similarly deep topics.

ONE DAY, CHILD…

WHEN I WAS LITTLE, I would sneak out of Big Mama's house and go down the hill to the juke joint to spy on my uncle grinding with his girlfriend to The Ohio Players' "I Want to Be Free" and Earth, Wind & Fire's "Reasons."

They didn't make it as a couple—and there were probably a number of reasons for that—but when I got older and looked at the lyrics to those songs, I realized they didn't stand a chance in hell.

QUARANTINE, DAY 21

HE LOVED mornings when the sun trickled through his blinds. Before everything shut down, he'd never paid attention to how the weather affected his moods. The sun was now an indicator that something about the world was still normal, beautiful.

He reached for his notebook and began to write.

Maybe today he would call someone.

HORNS

22

D ENNIS USED to carry around a trumpet (no case), just one hand on his horn and the other on his johnson. No one had actually seen him play it before, but he held it with such a confidence we just assumed he was an expert.

I guess the same could also be said for his johnson.

I AIN'T NEVER DID THIS BEFORE
(AFTER J. COLE)

AFTER MONTHS OF PLEADING, Devon got his wish. Angie had agreed to come over while his parents were out of town.

That afternoon he went to the pharmacy and tip-toed to the prophylactic section. Fearing all eyes were on him, he grabbed the first box he saw and ran to the register before the cashier could see him blush.

Later when Angie came over, they sat side-by-side on his bed as he opened them.

Non-lubricated was an understatement. They looked cornstarchy like surgical gloves.

"Any lubricant?" she asked.

Just spit, he thought, shrugging.

"Well, then I hope you brought your appetite," she said.

TIGER STRIPES

IF LEFT to his own devices, Rico would wax poetic for hours about pitching woo to redbones. He was single, he bragged, because he didn't want to tie himself down. He was an explorer, on the constant quest for poontang.

Family and friends kept telling him to slow his roll, to settle down, have a few big-headed crumb snatchers, make an honest woman out of one of those single women at the church, but he said, "No way."

He grew old and moved into a retirement community, where he continued hunting tail for the rest of his days.

When he was finally laid to rest, he was buried with a fedora, a herringbone chain, and the last of his Viagra prescription.

UBER PATIENT

THEY WERE REALLY GOING to do it. Tony wanted to say something to stop them from fucking all over his backseats, precious bodily fluids all in the fabric that he'd have to clean up later, time wasted that could have been used to drive more customers.

But they were an attractive couple—and his curiosity got the better of him—so he let it happen.

Later, when he was scrubbing his backseat, he cursed them beneath his breath. All of that, and those motherfuckers had still given him three stars and a lousy tip.

FRUIT

HE FELT stupid for spending the last of his money on a pack of seeds, but he was desperate for companionship. He decided to plant just one —in case this thing actually worked.

That one seed grew into a rather large plant, where the fruit appeared to grow even larger, slowly taking human form. Once it ripened, it fell off, and he unpeeled it to reveal a beautiful woman.

He looked at the remaining pack of seeds, now tempted, but she caught him looking and quickly grabbed the seeds and ate them, before ripping the plant to pieces.

He shrugged and smiled, satisfied to have the one. But she had no intention of staying, and promptly set off on her own.

IT WAS ALL A DREAM

THEY TOLD him it had been a dream, that his wife and daughter didn't really exist, that sometimes dreams just took hold of you like that.

He argued that he'd seen four birthdays and six anniversaries. Surely he couldn't have just made that up.

He considered whether there was some multiverse he had brushed against.

If there was, he would never find it, just like he would never dream of them again. He would have to resign himself to the fact that his life would be incredibly empty going forward.

HOOFING

FOR G.H.

THREE SCREWS FOR EACH TAP, two taps on each shoe, but all of that was enough for Gregory Hines to transform dance. He sang with Luther and danced alongside Baryshnikov and was always the baddest motherfucker in the room when folks wanted to flex their Capezios.

Me, I'm not much of a dancer these days, but occasionally I'll slap the ball of my foot against the floor and sweep it back before dropping my heel—a kind of call to the universe, hoping the beats will find Gregory smiling somewhere, his shoes ready to catch the beat and send it on into eternity.

THE OTHER SIDE OF THE BED

CARMICHAEL HAD WARNED Louise that he sometimes suffered from night terrors and therefore couldn't sleep on his back.

"The witch will come and sit on my chest," he told her.

Amused, she decided one night to push him onto his back as he slept.

Half an hour later, he began to scream in his sleep.

"The witch!" he mumbled, finding his words as he sat up in bed.

Louise pulled him into her arms and comforted him until he went back to sleep.

Prior to that moment, she didn't realize she had it in her to be both his savior and his tormentor.

DOPE

IT WAS A DOPE IDEA, the kind of idea anyone would be damn lucky to roll up on in a lifetime. The problem was that she didn't trust anyone, couldn't give a cripple crab a crutch. She just wasn't built that way. And since she didn't have the skills to pull it off herself, she wrote it down and locked the notebook inside the box where she kept her other dope ideas, hoping that one day when she was dead and gone, someone worthy enough would dig them up—and if the ideas were still dope—make them happen.

NEW AND BLUE

SHE WANTED to rock a pair of "Chicago" Jordan 1's with her wedding dress, but her maid of honor thought the red outline with the black swoosh would be too much for the white dress. Plus, it might send the wrong message for people who looked at those colors and immediately thought of the Devil.

She opted instead to buy a pair of "UNC" Jordan 1's. That way she'd only need something old and something borrowed.

WHAT THEY DIDN'T TELL HIM

THEY'D WARNED him about the shortage of sleep, the fact he'd probably have to try a few pediatricians until he found the right one, about the best strollers and cribs, soaps and even diaper disposal units. What they didn't tell him, though, was that he would spend hours happily lying on his stomach, discovering new ways to make his baby girl laugh.

WORK-IN-PROGRESS

WHEN I SEE SNOOPY CHILLIN' on top of his house, pecking away on his typewriter, I have to wonder if he ever finished his masterpiece. Or is he just going through the motions like the rest of us?

ACCULTURATING

HE REFUSED to call her by the anglicized name she'd given herself for co-workers who'd had trouble pronouncing her real name, and while he couldn't pronounce it like a native, she liked the fact that he tried.

In his mouth, her name sounded new and beautiful, like a song, something familiar, yet foreign at the same time.

In the States, she had no plans of abandoning her new name, but she still allowed him his attempts to conjure pleasant memories of home.

QUARANTINE, DAY 35

(AFTER ERNEST HEMINGWAY, OR THE NEWSPAPER ARTICLES THAT PRECEDED HIM)

FOR SALE: prom dress, never used.

HOW THEY BECAME LEGENDARY

MARZ BANX STEPPED to the mic, his stomach bubbling like some out of control science experiment. He glanced at Marvin the Martian, whose computer setup drew side-eyes from the old school DJs in the crowd, and nodded for the beat to drop.

They'd practiced this set a hundred times in their dorm room, but having an audience was different.

When the host had introduced them, he almost laughed at their name. "Up next, the—huh huh—Space Modulators." Definitely on some "Five Heartbeats/Bird and the Midnight Falcons" shit.

Marz grabbed the mic and proceeded to shut up the doubters—for the next twenty years.

MEMORIES OF A QUARANTINE

FIVE YEARS after moving to New York City, Lanette realized the primary way she was using her car was when she moved it from one side of the street to the other each week when the street sweepers came through.

She bought Metro cards, not gas. Still, she held on to the car and paid the insurance, just in case she ever needed to flee the city, again.

A SIDEWALK SUCCUMBS

WHETHER IT WAS bikes or skates or two-hand touch football games that got a little out of hand, all of the kids on 5th Street had made a sacrifice of their skin to the sidewalk. It was a rite of passage.

Decades later, when the last of the kids was gone, and there was no more blood trickling from knees or elbows or chins, now unable to stave off the weeds of neglect, the sidewalk shriveled up, cracked, and died.

EYES

(FOR ZOË)

WHEN SHE FINISHED EACH DOLL, she reached into a box of eyes, carefully selecting the perfect pair, before sewing them on. A nice finishing touch.

She'd never bought eyes before—in fact, she didn't know where they came from—but every time she opened the old box she'd purchased at the antique store, the eyes appeared.

So she continued to make the dolls, not because of any skill or passion for making them, but because she needed somewhere to put the eyes.

THE DANCE

TERRELL HAD NEVER SLOW DANCED with a girl before, but he put on his best rayon shirt and hit himself with a spritz of Cool Water before heading to the 1988 Daily High Homecoming Dance, hoping to get a dance with Tammy McClendon.

When Bobby Brown's "Roni" came on, he made his move.

"I don't dance to slow songs," she said, barely looking at him.

For the rest of the night, he leaned against the wall until the gym lights came on.

Heading out the door, someone grabbed his hand.

"Why didn't you come back and ask me to dance on a fast song?" She looked down awkwardly. "I've never really slow danced before."

PERSPECTIVE

IT WASN'T that he was fugly; he just didn't favor nobody.

QUARANTINE, DAY 43

(AFTER AUGUSTO MONTERROSO)

WHEN THEY AWOKE, the quarantine was still there.

THE KING OF GANGSTA FLATS

My TMJ started acting up when I was thirty wings in. The contest referred to them as "gangsta" because of how hard they were fried. To be competitive I had to eat at least fifty, but now that seemed more and more unlikely.

"Five minutes left," the announcer said.

I stared at the wing flat in my hand, not wanting to throw in the towel, but I could barely chew. I had thought, incorrectly, the hot sauce would soften them.

I resigned myself to failure, before tossing it back onto the plate.

What kind of prize was a t-shirt anyway?

AUTHORIAL LICENSE

To KEEP herself from writing under a pseudonym, Karen opted to use that name for the protagonist of her novel. As she worked on the book, she found herself writing herself more and more into the story, until finally she had come face-to-face with her character.

"Let's make a deal," the character said, smiling. "Why don't we switch names?"

Karen was almost too excited to respond. "Yes!"

In seconds she found herself knee-deep in the story's conflict, while somewhere way above her head, somewhere off the page, her character, Karen, began to orchestrate her existence.

ECLIPSE OF THE HEART

WHILE PERUSING the stack of used books on a table positioned along Third Avenue, Othario Johnson came across an anonymous battered old journal filled with entries from 1968-1969. He bought it for $5, then took it home to read.

He flipped to the April entries to read about MLK, but there was no mention of him. He then flipped to June. No mention of RFK. July 1969, no moon landing. Everything seemed to revolve around the author's brief romantic relationship with a woman who ultimately left her to pursue a career as an artist in Paris.

Othario lay down with the closed book on his chest, wondering what it would be like to have a love so strong it blocked out everything else in the world.

THE TAO OF KAP BAN

It was the kind of question a journalist might toss out there after the main interview was over: "If you weren't a successful rapper, what do you think you'd be doing?"

We'd been sitting in the studio for hours, Kap Ban steadily vaping between swigs of Budweiser, all the while cleaning pieces of his latest Glock.

He looked up, considering the question for a moment, then responded, "Probably a Buddhist monk."

"Seriously?"

"Yep. Been studying The Dharma for a few years now."

"I didn't think Buddhist monks did all of this," I said, nodding at various things around the room.

"Ever journey has to start from somewhere," he said, smiling.

THE SLEEP MONSTER

HE WAS afraid of hurting her in his sleep.

In the years before they met, he would wake to find that, somehow, he'd smashed his phone into the floor or had ripped apart a pillow, all while he thought he was sleeping peacefully. But back then, he'd lived alone. Now he was sharing his bed with someone else.

Those first nights he slept on his hands, waking the following morning with a spiky feeling tingling in his arms from poor circulation.

"Is something wrong?" she finally asked.

Not wanting to scare her, he responded, "No," then held her closely.

He'd planned to wait until she'd fallen asleep to pull back his arms and sleep on them, but when he awoke the following morning to find her safely snuggled in his arms, his eyes filled with tears of relief.

NUMBERS

JOSH ALWAYS WATCHED the lottery alone, his door locked to keep out his roommates. He'd been playing the same number for ten years, and after writing down Saturday's numbers, he checked his ticket against them ten times. He had thought if the moment ever came he'd scream, maybe dance. Now he sat holding his winning ticket, terrified.

$825,000,000.

What on earth would he do with that? And what about when his family and friends came for him? Could he trust anyone anymore?

He quickly endorsed the back of the ticket and quietly checked the internet for tickets to Australia.

ERIC'S THINGS, CIRCA 1985

ERIC'S FAMILY rolled into Tupelo like a tornado, and by sunset, Reggie was homeless.

The lawyer told Reggie since everything the couple had acquired was in Eric's name, legally Eric owned it, and without a will, the law dictated Eric's family would get the assets Reggie had contributed to over the years.

Reggie pleaded with them to keep a few things, like the Oldsmobile only he'd driven, but they denied him, as they had their son when he was alive.

They burned Eric's things and sold the house, but they could never find the car—although they had their suspicions.

QUARANTINE, DAY 51

HE LAY in bed all day, imagining that he was sinking into the mattress—beneath the mattress into the floor—beneath the floor into the Sunken Place.

His blinds drawn, darkness merging night with day, he was left only with his thoughts—and a phone that felt like a toy in a world where everything was suddenly more grown up.

DO THE WRITE THING

I MAY BE A CHARACTER, but I have feelings, too. You can't just take me and drop me into precarious situations, all in the name of a "hero's journey." You make everything so hard for me, obstacle after obstacle. Sometimes I just want to chill out. I'm sure you understand.

AUTUMN

THEY SAT on a bench near the middle of the park, the occasional leaf drifting down from the towering oak overhead.

"I love autumn," she said.

"I love *you*," he responded.

As a breeze brushed across their bodies, he drew closer to her.

"I could sit here forever," she said, gazing into the orange horizon.

"I could, too—but only if I could sit here with you."

She laid her head gently upon his shoulder, hoping her reluctance would fall away like leaves.

She knew she would never love him like autumn, but he didn't need to know that, yet.

THE GIFT

HER SISTERS BOUGHT her a wig of human hair as a gift before her first round of treatments, but it felt funny on her head, so she placed it on a foam stand and named it Annalise.

At night, long after her sisters had returned to their homes, she talked to Annalise. She told Annalise the things she couldn't bring herself to tell anyone else, the fears that haunted her.

And while Annalise never said a single word in response, when she got the update from her oncologist, she wanted Annalise, above all others, to hear the good news first.

A GOOD DEATH

HE HADN'T CONSIDERED what a "good death" might be, until a close friend died in a plane crash. He wouldn't allow himself to imagine that experience.

While he knew he couldn't control the inevitable, he wrote "good death" down on his bucket list, knowing he would never cross it off.

NAMES

IT WAS difficult for Aisha to believe anything Roosevelt said at that point.

Seriously, how could you profess to be a mega-fan of a rapper, but couldn't pronounce his name correctly?

If it *were* possible, she didn't feel Roosevelt merited the consideration. He'd probably mispronounce her name, too, she figured.

DAMN YOU, ROGER GOODELL

I HAD ALREADY DECIDED if my name got called in the first round I wasn't going to be one of those dudes climbing all over the commissioner.

But then he actually called my name.

There I was, center stage, hugging him with tears in my eyes, like he was my father returning from back-to-back tours of duty.

I guess the moment just got the better of me.

PROTEST IN THE TIME OF COVID

As THE PREVIOUS night's fires mixed with the morning fog, Alex put on his face mask and went out to retrieve his morning newspaper from the driveway.

His street was quiet, peaceful, untouched.

Inside his home, his wife and son slept upstairs, oblivious to the fire still raging within him.

TUBA

It wasn't sexy, but she wanted him to serenade her at their wedding. So he hoisted the shimmering sousaphone over his shoulder, aiming it at the front doors of the church.

When she stepped into the sanctuary, he put the mouthpiece to his lips and began to play "She's Your Queen to Be" from *Coming to America*. She smiled, struggling to hold in her laughter.

When she reached the altar, he put the horn down.

"I didn't think you'd really do it," she whispered, taking his hand.

"Well, now you know I'd do anything for you," he responded.

Laughter still dancing in their mouths, they turned to face the officiant.

THE MASTERPIECE

THE BOOK TOOK him three weeks to write, but he told them it took ten years.

TINY STORIES

HE WROTE TINY STORIES, the kinds of stories few people would even call stories. But he knew they were bigger than they appeared—like the little gelatin tablets that, when wet, expanded into colorful foam dinosaurs.

Surely these tiny stories were big enough, if only readers gave them space to grow.

ACKNOWLEDGMENTS

The stories "Numbers" and "Eric's Things, Circa 1985" appeared in *The Centifictionist*, Volume 1. "The Gift" appeared in *Friday Flash Fiction*. "Buckroe" appeared in *Microfiction Monday Magazine*. "Protest in the Time of Covid" appeared in *50-Word Stories*. Many thanks to Clara Ray Rusinek Klein, Gayle Towell, Tim Sevenhuysen and the other editors of these fine magazines.

***

I would like to thank my beautiful wife, Lauren, and my wonderfully inquisitive daughter, Zoë. You are the reasons I write.

I would like to also thank Torrey Walker, Sabin Duncan, Nikki Williams, Mitchell Davis and the entire team at BiblioLabs, and all of the librarians who continue to embrace me and my work.

Finally, I would like to tip my hat to Phonte Coleman, Ana María Shua, Lydia Davis, Paul Strohm, and César Aira, inspirations for the form I used to write this book.

ALSO BY RAN WALKER

B-Sides and Remixes

30 Love: A Novel

Mojo's Guitar: A Novel / (Il était une fois Morris Jones)

Afro Nerd in Love: A Novella

The Keys of My Soul: A Novel

The Race of Races: A Novel

The Illest: A Novella

Bessie, Bop, or Bach: Collected Stories

Four Floors (with Sabin Prentis)

Black Hand Side: Stories

White Pages: A Novel

She Lives in My Lap

Reverb

Work-In-Progress

Daykeeper

Most of My Heroes Don't Appear On No Stamps

Portable Black Magic

The Strange Museum: 50-Word Stories

Bees + Things + Flowers: Microfictions

ABOUT THE AUTHOR

Ran Walker is the author of twenty books. He is the winner of the 2019 Indie Author of the Year and 2019 BCALA Fiction Ebook Awards. He teaches creative writing at Hampton University and lives with his wife and daughter in Virginia. He can be reached via his website, www. ranwalker.com.